Janet Lawler

If Kisses Were Colours

Illustrated by Alison Jay

templar publishing

For Andy and Cami
J.L.

For Anne with love
A.J.

If kisses
were colours . . .

If kisses were colours, you'd see every one

of the bands of a rainbow that shines in the sun.

If kisses were pebbles, your beach would be lined

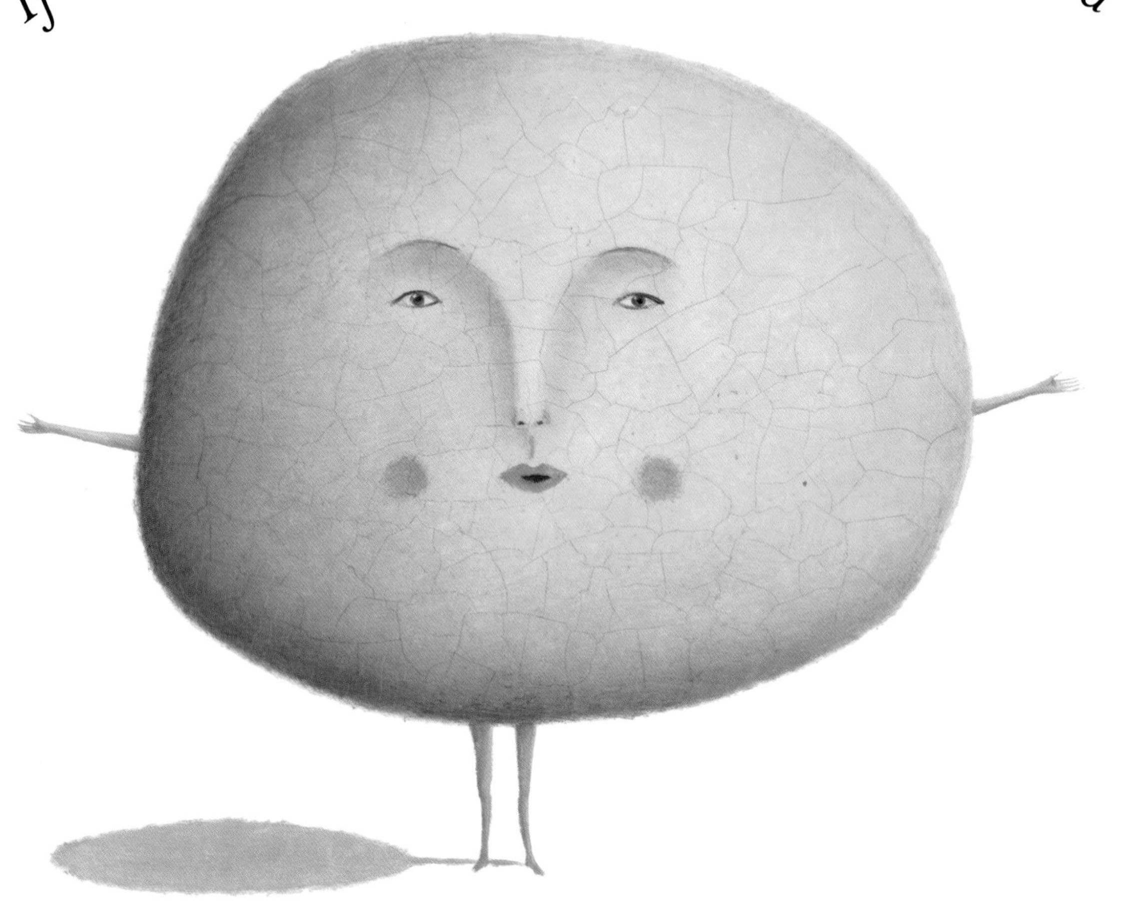

with stones by the millions, of all shapes and kinds.

If kisses were comets, the sky would be bright

with flashes of fire that streak through the night.

If kisses were flowers, you'd have huge bouquets

of roses and daisies

picked fresh every day.

If kisses were raindrops, a sea would appear,

created by showers that fall far and near.

If kisses were acorns, a forest would grow

of beautiful oak trees, in row after row.

If kisses were snowflakes, your world would be light,

sparkling with crystals of silver and white.

If kisses were blankets,
you'd always be warm,

wrapped up from the cold
during winter's worst storm.

My kisses are colours, and raindrops that flow,

and pebbles, and acorns, and comets that glow,

and flowers, and snowflakes that fall from above;

they're my way, sweet baby,
to give you my love.